SEAL

THE ALPHA ELITE SERIES

SYBIL BARTEL

BOOKS BY SYBIL BARTEL

The Alpha Elite Series
ALPHA
VICTOR
ROMEO
ZULU

The Alpha Bodyguard Series
SCANDALOUS
MERCILESS
RECKLESS
RUTHLESS
FEARLESS
CALLOUS
RELENTLESS
SHAMELESS
HEARTLESS

The Uncompromising Series
TALON
NEIL
ANDRÉ
BENNETT
CALLAN

The Alpha Antihero Series
HARD LIMIT
HARD JUSTICE

HARD SIN
HARD TRUTH
The Alpha Escort Series
THRUST
ROUGH
GRIND

The Unchecked Series
IMPOSSIBLE PROMISE
IMPOSSIBLE CHOICE
IMPOSSIBLE END

The Rock Harder Series
NO APOLOGIES

Join Sybil Bartel's Mailing List to get the news first on her upcoming releases, giveaways and exclusive excerpts! You'll also get a FREE book for joining!

SEAL

Navy SEAL.

Team Leader.

Warrior.

Men are born. Warriors are made. Honor is earned.

I was sixteen years old when I first heard those words from my best friend's father. The Vice Admiral took me in, taught me about integrity, and gave me what I'd never had—a family.

But it wasn't just my best friend and his father who changed my life.

The emerald-eyed blonde with an innocent smile stopped me dead in my tracks. Wanting to be a man worthy of her, I enlisted and became a SEAL. Except not even the Trident I'd earned changed the fact that she was the Vice Admiral's daughter and my best friend's much younger sister. She was strictly off-limits.

Then tragedy struck, and I found myself in the one position I never should've let happen—with my arms around her. Now I had one objective.

Code name: Alpha.
Mission: Retreat.

SEAL is a prequel to ALPHA, the first standalone book in the exciting Alpha Elite Series by USA Today Bestselling author, Sybil Bartel. Come meet Adam "Alpha" Trefor and the dominant, alpha Navy SEALs he serves with!

For my beloved son, Oliver.
You are still, and will *always* be my entire world.
I love you, Sweet Boy, and I miss you beyond words.

Oliver Shane Bartel 2004–2020

CHAPTER ONE

Adam

S TANDING SHIRTLESS AT THE KITCHEN SINK IN A PAIR OF SWEATS, I downed the glass of water as a small hand landed on my back.

"Couldn't sleep?" she asked like there was familiarity between us. "Come back to bed and I'll wear you out, sailor." Her lips touched my shoulder as her hand drifted to my abs and headed south.

I spun and grabbed her offending wrist. "Not a sailor." I was a SEAL. Not that I'd told her that, but my best friend and teammate, Billy, had told both her and her friend last night in the bar that we were Navy. The idea of a uniform had been enough for both of them.

It always was with women like her.

Not that I gave a damn. Sex was sex, and she was just another nameless means to an end.

"I thought you said you were in the Navy?" Pouting, she tried to lean her naked body into mine.

Ignoring her question, I held her away from me. "I have

1

an early morning." I didn't. "Time for you to go." Stepping back, I dropped her wrist.

"But Angie drove and I don't have a car," she whined, reaching for me again. "We have time for another round."

I didn't do second rounds, and I didn't do this. "Already told you last night what this was."

Finally cutting the act, she crossed her arms and dropped the higher pitched baby voice. "Seriously?"

Her fake breasts that were pushed together having zero effect on me, I didn't even glance at them. "Seriously."

"Oh my God, I'm standing here naked and you're really going to hang on to your *one and done* line you fed me at the bar?"

I really was. Not commenting, I gave her nothing except my locked expression.

"I take it back." She scowled. "You aren't the best sex I've ever had. You're just an asshole. I'm out of here." Spinning on her heel, she strutted toward my bedroom but yelled at my closed guest room door. "Angie! Let's go, we're leaving!"

I should've felt like a dick, but I didn't. She got hers, three times.

I was many things, but selfish in bed wasn't one of them.

No remorse for the angry woman banging on my guest bedroom door before she headed into my room, I leaned against my kitchen counter and fought the same damn bullshit in my head I fought every time I bedded a woman over the past year.

Bullshit I had no business thinking about.

But no matter how hard I tried, I couldn't wipe it clean.

Blonde hair and green eyes crept into my conscience like a fucking barometer for honor which was zeroing out with every additional thought I let slide into my screwed-up head.

If I had some respect, I wouldn't be thinking of her smile.

If I was a better man, I wouldn't be thinking about her at all.

But I was.

All the damn time.

Every time we came off a mission, she was the first person I wanted to call. The first and only voice I wanted to hear. The woman I wanted to come home for. But she wasn't a woman.

She was seventeen years old.

And she was my best friend's little sister.

Maila "Emmy" Marie Nilsen.

Fuck.

I shook away thoughts of her and the shit that was making me feel guilty as hell for fucking the woman tonight whose name I couldn't even remember.

Not that I remembered any of their names.

On purpose.

Because I didn't want to.

The Team was my focus and only one female mattered to me. The same one who'd mattered for the past eleven years.

Still leaning on the kitchen counter, my arms crossed, I

held position as the brunette walked out of my bedroom in her dress from last night with her purse slung over her shoulder, and her heels in one hand.

With an open palm, she banged against the guest bedroom's door again as she glared at me. "Angie, let's GO!"

A muffled moan came from the room before Billy chuckled and called out. "Angie's busy right now!"

The brunette's glare, still aimed at me, amped up like my best friend fucking her friend was my fault. "Don't make me bust this door down," she warned.

I thought about the two grand in security deposit I had on the place, wondering if I gave a damn if she kicked the door in.

I'd kicked so many doors down on missions, I'd lost count.

I glanced at the door. Then at the woman.

Definitely didn't give a damn.

Walking past her, I aimed for my bedroom and a hot shower to rinse off her cloying as fuck perfume.

"Where the hell do you think you're going?" she demanded.

I didn't answer.

Shutting my door, I cursed myself for not seeing this one coming. Women like her had tells. Tempers, clingers, Frog Hogs—they all had warning signs and I'd learned to spot them and avoid them. But last night, I'd apparently been off my game.

Who the fuck was I kidding?

I hadn't been off my game. My head wasn't even in the game. Squarely focused on a blonde back home in Miami, this was the precise reason why I hated these short bursts of downtime between missions and training. It wasn't enough time to catch a flight home, but twenty-four hours was too damn long to be obsessing about things I had no business thinking about.

Stripping my sheets and tossing them into a laundry basket in the closet, I grabbed a new set and dropped them on the bed. About to step out of my sweats to hit the shower, I heard my cell vibrate on the nightstand.

My pulse fucking kicked and I reached for the phone.

Only six people had my number, but none of them would call at oh-two-hundred. Not unless something was wrong.

Picking up my cell, I saw her name flash and my adrenaline spiked.

I answered immediately. "Emmy, what's wrong?"

Choking sobs filled my ear.

"Emmy, take a breath." Alarm spread and I was already grabbing a T-shirt. "Are you hurt? What's going on?"

"D-d-daddy," she stuttered, crying hard. "Adam, pl-pl-please. Wh-wh-wh-where's Billy? He-he's not answering. Y-y-you ha-have to h-help, Adam, *help me!*"

I rushed out of the bedroom and kicked in the guest bedroom door myself. Holding the phone to my ear as the door banged on its hinges, I spoke in a controlled calm I didn't fucking feel as Billy jumped off the woman he was fucking. "Emmy, sweetheart, take a breath, what's going on?"

"*Fuck*," Billy cursed, reaching for his boxers. "What's going on? Give me the phone, Alpha," Billy demanded.

"*D-d-daddy*," Emmy cried on a wail.

Holding my hand up to Billy, I spoke to Emmy. "What's wrong with your father, Emmy?"

"He-he-he's gone," she choked out. "*He died.*" The line filled with her gut-wrenching sobs.

CHAPTER TWO

Adam

MY HEART FUCKING STOPPED AS I LOOKED AT MY BEST FRIEND. "Emmy, listen to me, we're on our way. Billy's here with me. Who's with you right now? Where are you?"

"Hospital," she sobbed. "Pl-pl-please, *hurry.*"

"We're on our way." Her tears fucking killing me, I grabbed Billy's shoulder. "Here's your brother. Just hang tight, we're coming down." I held the phone toward him, but before I let go of it, I gave Billy words we both knew would do nothing. "It's your father. I'm so fucking sorry, brother."

Billy's face fell as he took the phone. "Emmy, what happened?" He listened for a second, then sunk to the bed and dropped his head into his hands.

I glanced at the chick he'd been fucking.

Standing on the opposite side of the bed, holding the sheet up in front of her, she looked like she'd seen a ghost. "What happened?"

"Both of you need to get out. *Now.*" Not giving her or

7

the other woman in the doorway a second fucking glance, I grabbed Billy's cell and scrolled the contacts.

As the girl grabbed her clothes, I dialed.

Our teammate and friend, Zane "Zulu" Silas, answered on the second ring. "I'm not fucking picking you up from some bar, asshole. If you're drunk, walk the fuck home. I'm busy." A woman giggled in the background.

"It's Alpha. How fast can you get your hands on a private plane?" Zulu had his private pilot's license before he'd joined the Navy, hell before he'd gotten his driver's license. "Billy and I need to get down to Miami ASAP." A commercial flight would take until tomorrow and I didn't want Emmy waiting for us to make the fourteen-hour drive from Virginia Beach to Miami.

"Is Emmy okay?" Zulu asked immediately. "What the fuck happened?"

Ignoring the irrational jealously that he was asking about her, I told him what I knew. "It's not her, it's the Vice Admiral."

"*Jesus Christ,*" he drew the two words out with the same tone I fucking felt deep. "How bad?"

"As bad as it gets." Emmy and Billy's mother had died before I met them. The Vice Admiral was their only living parent as well as their last remaining relative. "Can you get us in the air?" Zulu had told me once he co-owned a small plane, but I didn't know if he still had it. We'd been neck deep in back-to-back missions recently and none of us had had much downtime.

"Yeah, *fuck*. Let me make a call and see if my Cessna's available. How's Bravo?"

I glanced at Billy.

His head still in his hands, he was quietly talking to his sister.

"Holding it together." But a fourteen-hour drive would send him over the edge. His little sister was his world. "Make that call. Rent a plane if you have to. I'll foot the bill. We just need to get down there."

"Good copy. Give me two minutes. I'll call you back." Zulu hung up and Billy's cell rang almost immediately with an incoming call.

Glancing at the screen and seeing our CO, Lieutenant Commander Davis's number, I took the call. "Sir, it's Alpha."

"Put Bravo on the phone," Davis demanded.

"He's on another line talking to his sister."

Davis dropped his usual authoritative tone and audibly exhaled. "So he knows."

I walked out of the room. "We don't know much. I just got the call from his sister. She's too upset to give details. I'm trying to get us down to Miami. Any intel you have would be appreciated."

"I just got the call myself. Friend of mine is a surgeon down there at the Miami VA and happened to be on duty when the Vice Admiral was brought in by ambulance after collapsing. He was DOA. No cause determined yet, but the doc's guessing heart attack or aneurysm or something similar. Is someone with Bravo's sister? I know she's young."

"She's seventeen, sir, and I'm not sure. I couldn't ascertain that information which is why I'm trying to get us down there ASAP. I've called Zulu to see if he can take us so we don't have to wait for a commercial flight or transport."

"Understood. Do what you have to do, Alpha. I'm clearing you, Bravo and Zulu for leave. I'll come down myself when you know the arrangements. This is going to hit the ranks hard. The Vice Admiral was well known and respected. He made an impact on a lot of lives."

"Agreed, sir." The Vice Admiral and his influence had changed my life.

Davis exhaled again then his tone filled with concern. "I've known Erikson Nilsen a long time, Alpha. He was a good friend. I also know your history with him and I know what you meant to him. He was proud of you. Damn proud. Same way he was proud of his own son. I know this must be hitting you as well. I'm sorry for your loss."

Years of training, and too much experience with loss, my tone stayed even. "Thank you, sir."

"Get Bravo down there. Call if you need anything. I'll be in touch."

"Ten-four."

Davis hung up.

I pulled my rucksack out of my closet and Billy's phone rang again.

"What'd you find out?" I asked Zulu.

"Cessna's fueled up and ready to go. Meet me at the Executive Airport, west entrance. I'm on my way now. We can be wheels up as soon as I do prechecks. Flight time is two hours. We'll get in before sunrise."

I threw clothes in my bag and grabbed my dress blues. "Good copy. I'm getting us packed up now. We'll be there in twenty."

"Ten-four. I'd be surprised if Davis hasn't already heard, but I'll call him."

"He just called." I grabbed some toiletries then dumped my bag by the front door. "He already knows and he's clearing you, me and Billy for leave."

"Copy that. See you in twenty."

"Thanks, Zulu, owe you."

Zane paused for a moment, then in a rare show of emotion, he let his guard down. "You don't have to ever fucking thank me, Alpha. We're brothers, man. I got your six."

"Brothers," I agreed.

CHAPTER THREE

Adam

BILLY SCRUBBED A HAND OVER HIS FACE AS I PULLED INTO THE private airport's west entrance.

"I can't fucking believe this. How the hell did this happen?" Billy looked at me with grief in his eyes. "He was only fifty-fucking-seven."

Shoving my own shit down, I glanced at him. "I wish I had a better answer, but I don't know."

The only thing I'd been acutely aware of since before I was old enough to vote was that none of us got out of this alive. We all had an expiration date. The only difference between any of us was what you decided to do with the time you had.

"Fuck, Alpha, is this what you've had to deal with all these years? No parents, no relatives?"

"You have Emmy." *We* had Emmy.

"That's not what I meant. My sister's my world. You know that. But beyond that, I mean a whole family. You have none."

I had him and Emmy. And I used to have the Vice Admiral. In my mind, they were my family. I didn't talk about the shit I'd been born into, and I sure as fuck didn't dwell on the past. The eleven years I'd had with the Vice Admiral was worth more than a hundred lifetimes compared to what I'd come from. The only thing my drug-addicted, biological mother taught me was that blood relations meant nothing. I'd learned early on that fending for myself meant that you either pushed through and kept living, or you went down as a nameless, faceless coward that no one would remember, let alone give a shit about after you drew your last breath.

I wasn't going to be that coward, and Billy couldn't even if he tried. William "Billy" Nilsen was the bravest fucking SEAL on our team. Sometimes reckless, most times headstrong, but always fucking fearless, he was a goddamn warrior. I knew without reservation he would survive.

"We'll get through this," I promised.

Billy shook his head like he couldn't believe this was happening despite what we saw every damn day downrange. "Maybe I don't want to get through this. It seems like we lose brothers every fucking deployment and now my dad's dead, and I'm wondering what the hell we're doing."

I pulled into a parking spot and looked at him. "We're

getting to Emmy. That's what we're doing. Three foot world, brother."

"We're not on a motherfucking op, Adam." He spit out my real name with an impotent rage I knew all too well. "This is life. This is death. It's not the fucking Navy."

"Vice Admiral Erickson Nilsen *was* the Navy." He lived and breathed for his service to his country. "This is no different. Focus up. Stay mission objective."

His fight left him and he leaned back. "Yeah, and what fucking mission is that? Bury another body?"

Pissed that Emmy was alone, mad at the injustice in this world that took the good men too early, I didn't placate my best friend. "The mission is to get to your seventeen-year-old sister as fast as fucking possible so she's not going through this alone."

Inhaling deep and closing his eyes, Billy exhaled but then he slammed his fist into the passenger side of my truck three times in rapid succession. *"FUUUCK."* Emotion choked his roar of grief and he covered his face with his hands.

I grabbed his shoulder.

"I'm good." He jerked out of my hold. "I'm fucking good. I got it. You're right. Let's get to my sister." Grabbing his bag, he threw his door open.

Reaching for my own bag, I followed him across the apron to the only plane with lights on in the middle of the night at the private airport.

Looking up from his prechecks, Zulu circled the small Cessna and came at us. With a shake of his head, he grabbed Billy's shoulder. "I'm sorry, brother. So fucking sorry."

"Thanks." Billy shook him off, then inhaled deep and ground out his next words. "Appreciate the ride."

"Like I told Alpha, you don't have to thank me, Bravo. This is what we do." Zulu tipped his chin toward the plane. "Come on, we're ready to go." Zulu took Billy's bag and stowed it in the back of the Cessna.

I handed my bag over to Zulu, then glanced at Billy. "Did you let Emmy know we're wheels up?"

Billy just stood there staring at the plane for a moment. Then he looked at me. "Have you ever heard her like that?" Inhaling, he shook his head. "I don't know if I can hear that again right now."

I knew exactly what he meant. Her crying had fucking crushed me. "I'll let her know we're on our way."

"Before we left your apartment I tried calling her back, but she didn't answer."

I tamped down the urge to fucking throttle him, and ask why the hell he hadn't tried her again. We were SEALs. We didn't fucking break, and we didn't back down when shit went FUBAR. We worked the goddamn problem. Emmy needed that from us. She deserved our best, especially right now.

Checking my tone, I asked what I needed to know. "Did you make sure someone was with her?"

"Yeah." Billy scrubbed a hand over his face. "The neighbor, Mrs. Jansen, was there with her at the hospital. She said she'd take her home and stay with her until we got there."

"I'll take care of it." I pulled my cell out. "Get on the plane."

Billy nodded and stepped aboard, taking one of the rear passenger seats.

I sent a quick text.

Me: *Emmy, I'm calling right now. Answer for me, please.*

I dialed.

The phone rang three times before her voice, small and devastated, breathed one word. *"Adam."*

I wanted to reach through the phone and grab her and take her into my arms. The urge to call her a term of endearment overwhelming, I refrained. "I'm right here, Emmy. Billy, me and Zane are on our way down. Zane's flying us. Flight time is about two hours. Do you have someone with you right now?"

"The doctor at the hospital made me take something," she whispered in the same hoarse, grief-stricken voice.

My jaw ticked. "What did they gave you?"

"I don't know." She sniffled. "Xanax, I think." Her voice got even quieter. "But it's not working. I can't stop the tears."

"You're not supposed to right now, sweetheart." Fuck holding back what I should or shouldn't call her. "I'm coming for you, honey. Billy too. We're just a couple hours out. I need you to hang on until then, okay? Can you do that for me?"

She sniffled. "You never call me sweetheart."

"Not out loud," I selfishly admitted. "Maybe it's time I start."

"*Adam*," she whispered, stifling a small cry.

"We're almost there, sweetheart. Hang on for me."

She let the small cry escape. "I'll try."

I was so fucking thankful she wasn't hysterically crying but I didn't like the utter defeat I heard in her voice either, not that I could blame her. "Who's with you, baby?"

"Mrs. Jansen," she whispered.

I exhaled, marginally relieved. "Good. Is she close to you right now?"

"Yes."

"Okay, I'm going to have you put her on the phone, but first tell me you understand that we'll be there in two hours."

"Two hours," she repeated in a voice so small, it broke me.

"On our way, sweetheart. Hang on. Put Mrs. Jansen on now for me, okay?"

"Okay, but Adam?"

"Yeah, baby?"

"*Hurry,*" she whispered before I heard the shuffling of the phone.

A second later, the elderly neighbor came on the line. "Hello?"

"Mrs. Jansen, this is Adam Trefor. I wanted to let you know that Billy and I are on our way. We're flying down, so we'll be there in approximately two hours. I would appreciate it if you stayed with Emmy until we got there."

"Of course, dear. I'm not leaving her."

"Thank you. See you soon." I ended the call as Zulu fired up the Cessna's engines.

CHAPTER FOUR

Adam

J UST BEFORE OH-FIVE-HUNDRED, I PULLED THE RENTAL INTO THE
driveway of a home I knew better than my own growing
up. The Vice Admiral's car was parked next to the beater
Emmy had bought herself last year, and everything looked
normal.

But not a damn thing felt normal.

Zulu spoke from the backseat. "We got your six, Bravo.
Whatever you need from us, we're here."

"I just need to get to my sister," Billy muttered, pushing
his door open.

I followed Billy, and Zulu followed me. Without knock-
ing, Billy opened the front door and we all stepped into the
darkened entryway.

A cry, followed by Emmy's voice, broke the deafening
silence. *"Billy."*

Dumping his bag, Billy rushed into the living room and
caught his sister in his arms.

The moment he did, Emmy burst into hysterical sobbing and her legs gave out.

A lamp turned on as Billy held his sister in his embrace and Mrs. Jansen rose from the couch with effort.

"Fuck, Alpha," Zulu muttered behind me. "That girl's tears are gonna be the death of me."

Throwing him a warning look over my shoulder, I made my way to Mrs. Jansen and held my hand out. "Thank you for taking care of Emmy until we got here."

"Navy SEAL or not, I have known you since you were a teenager, Adam Trefor. You give me a hug."

"Yes, ma'am." I didn't do hugs. I didn't do affection, period, but this woman had my gratitude and she deserved respect. Leaning down, I was intent on keeping it as brief as possible when the older woman pulled me into her arms and held on tight as she whispered in my ear.

"I'm sorry for your loss, dear. I know what he meant to you, and you to him."

"Thank you, ma'am." Uncomfortable, I pulled away. "Can I take you home so you can get some sleep?"

I no sooner asked and Emmy said my name on a gut-wrenching wail. "*Adam.*"

Mrs. Jansen's hand patted my arm. "Take care of our girl. I'll see myself home."

She didn't have to tell me, I was already front and center, taking Emmy into my arms as Billy reluctantly released her.

Her soft curves and strawberry-smelling hair landed

against me as her arms went around my neck and suddenly I was inhaling for the first time in as long as I could remember.

Stroking her back, feeling her grief as her small body shook with sobs, I held her like I'd never held anyone else—tight and to my heart. "Shh, Emmy. We're here. It's going to be okay."

She cried harder.

I looked over the top of her head at Billy.

His eyes on her, he stood there like he didn't know what the fuck to do.

I got it.

Neither of us handled it well when she was hurt or sad, but this was unprecedented, and of all the shit that was flying through my head, there was one key fact that stood out above all else. A fact I was sure was going through Billy's head.

Emmy was seventeen and now parentless.

But God help me, the Emmy in my arms didn't feel seventeen.

Her breasts pressed to my chest, her hips flaring from a small waist, her hair soft and everywhere, she was a teenager in a woman's body. A teenager who'd just lost her last living parent.

Stroking her back once more, I pulled away just enough to look down at her. "Have you eaten?"

Tears sliding down her face and soaking my T-shirt, she shook her head.

Reluctantly, I grabbed her waist and started to hand her

over to Billy. "Sit with Billy, I'm going to make you something to eat, then we're all going to try to get a few hours of sleep."

"Alpha," Zulu called from the foyer. "I'm taking Mrs. Jansen home. Be back in ten."

"Copy." Lifting Emmy's now limp arm from around my neck like she'd given up on holding on to anyone, I placed it around her brother's shoulders. But then I slipped in front of my best friend. "Billy's got you, sweetheart."

Looking more grief-stricken than before we'd walked into the house, Billy seemed to miss what I'd called his little sister as he took her from me and sat them both down on the couch.

Immediately curling into his side, Emmy let loose with a fresh wave of tears.

Forcing myself not to look back at her, I walked into the kitchen.

Ten minutes later, I was plating grilled cheese sandwiches when Zulu walked into the kitchen.

"I called the hospital, said I was Bravo, got the run around at first, but finally was put through to someone in administration. The Vice Admiral's in the morgue. The ME is going to perform the autopsy later this morning, then his body should be released for whatever funeral home they want to use. Do you know if there were any prearrangements made? Is he going to Arlington?"

Unfortunately, all of us on the Teams were well versed in the drill of what happens after someone dies and even more familiar with making arrangements. "Negative on Arlington.

They have a family plot here in Miami. I know he wanted to be buried with his wife. We can ask Billy which funeral home. Knowing the Vice Admiral, there's something already lined up." I handed Zulu a plate.

"Copy that." Taking the food, Zane looked down. "Grilled cheese? Seriously? What am I, five?"

"It's Emmy's favorite." Picking up the rest of the plates, I walked into the living room as the sun started to rise.

CHAPTER FIVE

Adam

STANDING IN THE UPSTAIRS HALL, I WATCHED MY BEST FRIEND back quietly out of his sister's bedroom. "She asleep?"

Billy silently closed her door. "Yeah. For now."

Leaning against the wall in the upstairs hallway, I eyed my best friend. "How are you holding up?" It'd been a long couple of days. The wake had been tonight and tomorrow was the funeral.

Billy shook his head. "Who the fuck has an aneurysm at fifty-seven?"

According to the ME, apparently his father, but I didn't say shit because there were no words that undid death. We both knew the drill. None of us walked out of this alive. Losing too many brothers downrange only brought that fact home, but losing family was different.

Billy slumped against the wall. "What am I going to do about her? Emmy's not even eighteen. I can't leave her, but I can't not go back."

This was the third time we'd had this conversation and I

repeated the same thing I'd been saying all along even though it felt so fucking wrong, it was eating a damn hole in my stomach. "Between the housekeeper and Mrs. Jansen, she won't be alone. We'll come home between deployments. Next year she'll be in college. She already told you she doesn't want to move up to Virginia Beach." We'd both asked, repeatedly. Emmy had been adamant about staying in the house and finishing her senior year. She'd said it was what their father would've wanted, and I didn't disagree. "You know she's a hundred times more mature than we were at her age." With all the deployments the Vice Admiral had been on, Billy and Emmy had practically raised themselves anyway. "She'll stay focused up."

Billy scrubbed a hand over his face. "I'm not worried about her fucking off at school." He met my gaze. "I'm worried about her being alone."

I didn't have an answer because I was having the same damn thought.

But more than all the years I'd helped her with a skinned knee, or put her to bed, or made her grilled cheese, I was now thinking about the girl who'd grown into a woman's body since the last time I'd seen her and I was worried about a hell of a lot more than her being alone.

If the stream of prick teenager dudes coming by to give their condolences was any indication, I wasn't the only one noticing how she'd grown into a beautiful young woman.

"Fuck." Billy pushed off the wall. "Tomorrow's gonna suck."

"Me and Zulu got your back. Whatever you need, let us know."

Dark circles under green eyes that matched his sister's, my best friend looked at me and for the first time in twelve years, I saw something on him I never saw.

The same shit we saw downrange.

Defeat.

In stark contrast to the sixteen-year-old with a quick smile, easy laugh and fucking eternally optimistic attitude, the man who stared back at me now wasn't that kid. Even after all the shit we'd seen as SEALs, all we'd done and been through, Billy had never lost his sense of humor, even during our worst fucking missions. Retaining his positive outlook on life, I'd never understood how he could crack jokes when shit went FUBAR, but he had.

Except I wasn't looking at that man now.

Like looking in the mirror, the weight of his gaze said it all.

"I'm sorry." The sentiment useless, I said it anyway.

"I know, man. I know." He slapped my shoulder as he walked past me to his room. "Thanks for being here for me and Emmy."

A flash of realization hit me square in the chest. He couldn't have kept me from Emmy this week. No fucking way. Keeping the thought to myself, feeling like I needed to get my head on straight, I tipped my chin. "See you in the morning."

"Yeah." Billy shook his head. "Tomorrow." He walked into his room and shut the door.

Like a fucking creeper, I stood there outside Emmy's room and listened for a long moment.

Not hearing her tears, I gave it another minute then turned toward the stairs. Before I made it one step, her voice, muffled and small, came through her bedroom door.

"Adam?"

My heart jumped to attention and my pulse fucking followed. No hesitation, I opened her door and scanned the room out of habit. Curled in her bed, the lights off, I could smell the sweet scent of sleep on her, but more, I could taste the weight of her grief. Grief I wanted to shoulder so bad, I thought about taking her into my arms and holding her all night.

Then I thought about the consequences of crawling into her bed and I put a red fucking light on that shit, locking my thoughts down tight. "What's wrong?"

Her inhale cut across her room and landed on the part of my chest only she could touch. "You have to do something for me."

Anything. "What?"

"Make sure he goes back."

For a full beat, I stood there.

I stood there and absorbed her words and I processed them. Looking for tells, listening for intonation, scanning the familiar furniture and layout in the ambient light from the moon—I paid attention to every single detail.

Because a seventeen-year-old who'd been through what she had didn't make that kind of request.

But Emmy wasn't a teenager.

Not anymore.

"Adam?"

"I heard you."

"Make sure," she repeated, her voice stronger as she curled into an even smaller ball.

I didn't need to make sure.

The Navy owned us, but more, honor owned Billy. The same honor that owned his sister.

Nothing to say, I grabbed the door handle. "Goodnight, Emmy."

"Goodnight, Adam."

Closing the door behind me, I almost wondered who'd really been through BUD/S.

Maila Marie Nilsen was stronger than any SEAL I knew.

CHAPTER SIX

Adam

DRENCHED IN SWEAT, DRESSED IN ONLY RUNNING SHOES AND shorts, I quietly stepped out of the south Florida humidity as I crossed the threshold of the front door and walked into the cool air conditioning.

Aiming directly for the kitchen, I grabbed a glass off the drainboard and filled it with tap water.

I was downing my second glass when I heard her light footsteps.

"You went for a run?" Her voice sleep-rough and hoarse, she asked the question without any intonation.

I turned.

My gaze landing on her, I took in every detail in a nanosecond.

Sleep shorts, long legs, mussed hair, tank top, no bra.

Christ, no bra.

"I did." Turning, I filled my glass again.

"Ten miles?" she asked, almost casually as she moved toward the coffee maker.

"Seven." It was hot as fuck this morning and I'd gotten a late start. I didn't want to be gone when she woke up. She'd have to deal with that soon enough.

"Why?" She measured grounds into the filter.

"Why what?"

"Why only seven miles?" She took the coffee pot to the fridge and filled it with filtered water.

"Seven's not enough?"

"You usually run ten." She bent slightly as she poured the water, looking into the coffee maker's reservoir.

Fuck me, I stared at her ass. "How do you know how far I run?"

"How do you know grilled cheese sandwiches are my favorite?" She put the pot under the filter, set the coffee maker to brew and turned toward me. "How do we know anything about each other?"

I didn't answer, I watched her cross her arms.

"I know you as well as I know Billy." She looked at me with the same sad eyes as her brother. "You're my second."

"Second?" I stupidly asked, wondering when the last time I'd had a conversation with a woman my own age was.

She nodded. "Second brother."

In that moment, I didn't want to be her brother. "I only ran seven because I woke up later than I expected."

Inhaling and dropping her head as if she suddenly remembered what today was, she nodded.

"What would you like for breakfast?" Zulu had done a

grocery run yesterday and we had more bacon than all of us could eat in a week.

"You're going to cook?"

I nodded but her head was still down and she couldn't see me. "Yeah."

"Then nothing." She looked up at me. "Until you go shower."

If it was any other day, I would've smiled at her and hoped like hell I got her smile in return. Because that was what was missing.

Her smile.

The smile I'd grown addicted to since the first time I saw it twelve years ago.

Swearing to myself that I would make her smile again one day, I set my glass in the sink. "Decide what you want. I'll make it after I clean up." I turned toward the stairs.

"Adam?"

I glanced over my shoulder.

Looking small as fuck and like she needed me to protect her from everything this world could dish out, she held my gaze for a moment.

Then she whispered two words I didn't deserve. "Thank you."

With a clipped nod, I took the stairs two at a time.

As I reached the bathroom, Billy came out of his room and glanced at me. "You go running without me?"

"Didn't want to wake you."

He glanced across the hall at Emmy's open door. "She up?"

I tipped my chin then shifted my gaze. For the first time, I didn't want to talk about her with him. "Yeah."

"Zulu?"

"As far as I know, he's still asleep in the study downstairs." I'd given Zulu the pullout couch in the Vice Admiral's study and I'd taken the sofa in the living room. I normally didn't give a damn where I slept. Most places were nicer than the shit accommodations I'd dealt with the first sixteen years of my life. And after BUD/S, I'd learned to sleep standing up if I needed to check out for a few. But this trip, with everything going on, with all of us in the house, I hadn't given Zulu the study because I was being generous.

I'd taken the sofa because the living room was directly under her bedroom. If she got up in the middle of the night, I'd hear her.

And if I heard her, I was going to be there for her.

As if sensing my thoughts, Billy's gaze zeroed in on me. "How's Emmy this morning?"

Barely glancing at him, I toed off my running shoes. "In the kitchen making coffee."

"Why aren't you looking at me?"

My jaw ticked and I met his gaze directly. "Taking my shoes off, Bravo. That's all."

His eyes narrowed. "You never call me Bravo."

I did in the field. Always. Just like he called me Alpha.

"I'm hitting the shower. I'll make breakfast when I'm done."
I walked into the bathroom, but before I could close the door,
he stopped me in my tracks.

"Don't walk around shirtless in front of my sister
anymore."

"Copy that." Making him a promise I didn't know if I
could keep, I shut the bathroom door.

CHAPTER SEVEN

Adam

BILLY STOOD AT THE FRONT DOOR, SAYING GOODBYE TO THE last guests to finally fucking leave. The funeral had been packed, but all the people that'd come to the house with food afterward had felt even more crowded.

Dishes littering every square inch of counter space in the kitchen and dining room, I didn't know what the fuck we would do with it all.

Shutting the front door, Billy leaned back against it like he needed the support. "Zulu gone?"

"Yeah." Lieutenant Commander Davis, Zane, and all our teammates had left directly after the service because we were being spun up earlier than we thought. The Lieutenant did what he could for me and Billy to delay, but even that didn't buy us much more time. We had to report back tomorrow by eighteen-hundred hours. After that, we were wheels up for what Davis promised would be a long deployment.

Staring at the open door to the Vice Admiral's study, Billy exhaled. "Where's Emmy?"

"Kitchen. I'll start the clean-up."

With barely a nod, Billy pushed off the door and went into his father's study. A second later, he came out with a bottle of Jack. Aiming for the back door, he disappeared into the backyard without a word.

Walking into the kitchen, I quickly scanned the mess, but then my gaze fell on the blonde-haired, emerald-eyed young woman who'd been quiet and composed throughout the entire day.

Her black dress hugging every curve, her heels making her inches taller, she stood in the middle of the kitchen and took in all the dishes of food. Even with dark circles under her eyes and grief weighing down her expression, she was beautiful.

So goddamn beautiful.

Before I could stop it, her real name, not her nickname, was coming out of my mouth with a tone of dominance I had no fucking business using on her. "Maila."

Her gaze met mine and for a split second, every damn thing in the world suspended.

Then she burst into tears.

I didn't think.

I was on her faster than I had a right to be, pulling her into my arms and holding her so goddamn tight, I never wanted to let go.

Kissing the top of her head, I fed her bullshit lies. "Shh, it's okay. I'm here. Everything's going to be all right."

She cried harder, and the place in my chest reserved only for her fucking fractured.

"I got you." I kissed her soft hair again as an unfamiliar perfume I'd never smelled on her ghosted around me. The scent, warm and exotic, fucked with my head and went straight to my dick. "It's okay, baby." My hand ran down her long hair before settling on the small of her back and rubbing tight circles. I held her closer. "Shh, I got you. You're going to be okay."

"How?" she cried. "How did this happen? How do I do this?" Her tears soaked my dress blues.

"You're not alone. I will always be here for you, Maila. *Always.*"

Her tears turned into gut-wrenching sobs. "But you're going back."

Her tears destroying me, the desolation in her voice killing me, I gripped the sides of her face. Before I knew what I was doing, I was looking into her eyes like I wasn't a second brother to her. My heart rate going fucking rogue, I stared at her like she was mine.

Then the reality of the moment hit me and for the first time since I'd enlisted, I wondered what the hell I was doing.

This woman, this girl, she didn't need a Navy SEAL.

She didn't need a deployed brother.

And she sure as hell didn't need a father who was now buried next to her mother.

She needed someone who would be there for her.

Lost in her eyes, experiencing a weight on my chest I didn't know how to breathe through, I opened my fucking mouth. "Maila Marie Nilsen, I'm making you a promise."

Her entire body flinched. "Don't you dare go down that road with me, Adam." She wrenched out of my grip. "Do *not* make me promises." She swiped at her face. "Don't do it. Not now, not ever. As long as you wear that uniform, we both know what this is." Making an about-face, she walked out of the kitchen, but before she disappeared around the corner, she looked over her shoulder at me and made a mockery of everything I'd ever thought about bravery. "Serve your country, Adam. Honor that Trident, and keep you and my brother safe."

I was still standing in the middle of the kitchen when her bedroom door upstairs slammed shut.

A second later, her muffled crying drifted down from the second floor.

My hands fisted, my jaw ticked and I fought from taking the stairs two at a time, but she was right. I never should've opened my mouth.

She deserved better.

Better than any empty promise I could give her while I wore the uniform.

Shoving down impotent rage and my own selfish feelings of loss, I did what I had to do. What I always fucking did.

I took my jacket off, rolled up my sleeves and I fucking pushed through.

CHAPTER EIGHT

Emmy

UNABLE TO STOP THE TEARS, I TRIED TO MUFFLE MY CRIES into my pillow, but that only made his scent stronger. Even in his dress blues, Adam's masculine scent smelled like the cold wind of unattainable dreams and the sharp angles of stoic disconnectedness.

Cold wind and sharp angles.

That was Adam.

My Adam.

Except he wasn't my anything.

He was a Navy SEAL and my brother's best friend. Not to mention Daddy had taken Adam in the second he'd laid eyes on him like Daddy knew the boy with the worn-through sneakers and a stark look in his eyes needed us.

But I'd never thought Adam needed us.

Instead, I'd always thought we needed him.

I needed him.

Because the moment he walked into our house twelve years ago, it felt like the pieces of a puzzle had fallen together.

Then Adam had grown into a man so handsome and so austere that my heart never had a chance. I knew I was only seventeen and he was twenty-eight, and I shouldn't be thinking about his arms around me in the kitchen just now.

But I was.

Lord save me, I was. And I was doing it on the very day of Daddy's funeral. I was also selfishly thinking that I didn't want Billy or Adam to go back. I wanted to hold on to both of them forever, and never have them on the front lines again, but I knew how this life worked. I'd been painfully aware my whole life how the Navy worked.

You didn't serve without honor.

To ask my own brother, let alone Adam, to leave that service, that commitment they'd each made—I might as well ask them to commit treason.

I couldn't do it.

I wouldn't do it.

I had to be brave.

Daddy had always told me this day would come. That I would eventually be without him. He'd told me that I'd have to be strong when that happened, and stand proud on my own two feet knowing my father had lived a life of purpose. Except Daddy had always implied his end would come while he was in service to our country. He made it sound like he'd go down in a blaze of glory for the very freedom Billy and I had had our whole lives. He'd always said there was no greater sacrifice a man could make.

Except that didn't happen.

Daddy deserved more than the indignity of collapsing and never waking up. But I couldn't change what was any more than I could stop my heart from breaking.

Both Mama and Daddy were gone now, and all I could do was pray they were together.

But I wanted to pray for more than that.

I wanted to pray that the stoic man downstairs who wore a Trident and had Mediterranean blue eyes would wake up tomorrow and decide not to go back to the very place that had made him a man.

I wanted to pray he would stay.

For me.

But I knew Adam would no more stay than my own brother would.

A fresh wave of tears shook me and I held the pillow tighter as I tried to ignore the real truth.

Even if Adam did try to stay, I wouldn't let him.

That same sense of duty and honor that had been ingrained into them by Daddy had also been ingrained into me.

I couldn't live with myself if I was the reason why Adam walked away from the Teams.

CHAPTER NINE

Adam

I DIDN'T SLEEP AND NEITHER DID SHE.

With dark circles under her eyes, she stood on the driveway barefoot. Her shorts showing every inch of her long, toned legs, she crossed her arms protectively around herself and glanced at my rental before looking at her brother. "You'll call when you get to Virginia Beach?"

Billy threw his bag in the backseat of the rental, then he reached for her. "Of course." Holding her close, he swayed with her in his arms. "I always call." He kissed the top of her head. "You know that."

"Every week," she replied, either agreeing with him or making sure he followed through on his promise.

"You know it." Billy held her tighter as I glanced at my watch.

Her voice small and quiet, Emmy turned her face into her brother's chest. "This next deployment's going to be a long one."

Looking over her, Billy met my gaze and lifted an eyebrow.

I shook my head once. I hadn't told her anything about our next assignment.

Billy rubbed his hand over her back. "It's just another deployment, Emmy. Nothing different than all the rest," he lied.

Pulling out of his arms, she leaned away from him with a knowing look. "Don't lie to me. Before he passed, Daddy told me what's going on. This isn't like all the other deployments. You're going to be gone for a long time, maybe a year. You probably won't even make it to my graduation."

"Of course I will." Placating her, Billy reached for his sister to hug her again.

Emmy stepped back and her finger came out as she pointed at Billy's chest. "I know you're going to be gone for a while this time, and no, Daddy didn't tell me any more than that. So you don't need to freak out about anything."

I didn't know whether I was more fucking appalled that the Vice Admiral had given her classified intel or fucking grateful that I was seeing something besides grief in her eyes.

Billy's hands went to his hips. "When it comes to you, I'll freak out about whatever the hell I want to freak out about. And for the record, Dad didn't have any more intel on whatever the Navy has planned for us next than our own O-I-C. So whatever you think you know, or don't know, about what's coming, forget it. We're just door kickers, Emmy. That's our job. We may be the tip of the spear, but even we don't always get advance notice of what we're doing. We go where we're aimed."

"Billy," she stated like she knew he was full of it.

"Calm in the chaos." Billy kept going like she hadn't said anything. "Eliminating targets and doing our duty." He leaned down and kissed her temple. "Making the world a better place by keeping you safe."

Letting out a heavy sigh, she shook her head. Then she surprised me. Instead of giving him shit, she put her arms around him and hugged him one more time. "Doing your duty," she agreed. "Never betray the Trident."

Muted by circumstance, Billy smiled. The first smile I'd seen on him in days. "You know it, sis." He touched his lips to the top of her head. "Just serving the country I love."

"I love you," she whispered.

"Love you back, sis." Roaring as he held her tight, he then released her and tipped his chin in my director. "Give Alpha some love. We gotta go."

As natural as if she belonged to me, she stepped into my embrace.

The warm sun on her skin, the scent of her strawberry shampoo, the faint hint of the perfume she'd worn yesterday—she smelled like home.

My home.

"You be safe," she whispered, burrowed against my chest like she could stay there forever.

Emotions I didn't allow surfaced, and I had to choke them

down. Lowering my voice, I asked a stupid fucking question that didn't have an answer, but one I wanted a reply to anyway. "Are you going to be okay?"

"If I'm not, I'll just call you."

Relief I had no right to feel, swamped me. "You better."

"I will." Her arms tightened around me but then she let go and put distance between us. "No goodbyes." She crossed her arms protectively around herself again. "You both know I hate them."

"No goodbyes," Billy echoed as he got in the rental.

I waited until I heard the car door shut. "Promise me," I demanded.

Her pretty emerald-eyed gaze held me captive for a full beat. But then she nodded and whispered the words I selfishly needed to hear. "I promise."

Taking in every inch of her in a single glance and committing it to memory, I nodded once and got behind the wheel. Still staring at her, I turned the engine over, but then I forced myself to look away as I put the car in gear.

Leaning back in his seat, Billy watched his sister stand in the driveway while I pulled away. When I turned the corner and he couldn't see her anymore, his gaze cut to me. "We're gonna be gone for a year."

"I know." Fuck, I knew. My grip tight on the steering wheel, leaving her had felt wrong.

"Goddamn it." He scrubbed a hand over his face. "I'm going to miss her graduation."

So was I.

And that almost felt fucking worse than leaving her.

Billy looked back out the window. "I should've moved her up to Virginia Beach with us. She could've stayed in your guest room until I found us a place up there."

"Taking her away from everything she knows wasn't the right move." Moving her into my apartment would've been an even worse move. Not that I didn't want her there.

"You're right." Shaking his head in resignation, Billy sighed. "She would've been pissed."

Royally fucking pissed. Emmy loved Florida as much as she loved her brother. "She needed to stay in the house." In her home.

"I know, but that doesn't mean I'm okay with leaving her here with Mrs. Jansen and a housekeeper. Not that it's any different than all the times Dad was gone."

"She'll take care of herself." I didn't know if I was telling him or reassuring myself.

"She always has. Strongest woman I know."

She wasn't a woman, she was still a teenager. Something I needed to fucking remind myself as I thought of her in those damn shorts and tank top.

"So how long do you think it'll take us to eliminate this terrorist cell we're slated to go after?"

My phone vibrated in my pocket. "As long as it takes for another one to form." Pulling it out, I glanced at the screen.

"I really fucking hope this deployment doesn't take as long as Davis is saying it'll take."

I didn't answer my best friend.

My heart fucking pounding, I stopped at a light and read the text a second time.

Emmy: *I miss you already. But I really miss the way you held me in the kitchen last night. Stay safe. XO*

CHAPTER TEN

Adam

Twelve Months Later

"E XFIL, EXFIL, EXFIL," I ORDERED THROUGH MY COMMS. Gunfire erupting everywhere, the partially collapsed building shook with another explosion.

"Copy," Zulu answered.

"Copy," Bravo barked.

"Fucking squirters," Echo warned, firing off more rounds. "North exit, couple dozen."

"South side too," Delta added. "I can't see how many."

"On my way, Echo." Running down the stairs, my sights aimed, I exited the west side of the building and turned north. "Command, do you have a visual on Delta's position?"

"Affirmative, Alpha," Command replied through my comms. "Heat signatures showing multiple hostiles exiting the building from north and south entrances. Three vehicles approaching from the main access road."

"Securing hostage and coming your way, Delta," Bravo interjected.

"Good copy, Command," I answered, taking position at the northwest corner of the building behind a small shed before I glanced back at the road. "I have visual. Two trucks with vehicle mounted weapons, one armored SUV." Who the fuck knew how many more hostiles. "Hot extraction. We need new exfil coordinates."

"Coming up on your six, Echo." Zulu ran to Echo's position and started firing.

"Copy that, Alpha," Command replied. "Hold position for new coordinates."

"Squirters retreating into the building," Echo stated.

Fucking good. "Delta, charges set?"

"Set and ready to blow," Delta replied.

"Zulu, retrieve the hostage," I ordered.

"Already on it," Zulu responded.

Then we were out of here. "Northwest corner of the building, retreat, retreat, retreat," I ordered my Team before replying to Command. "Negative on holding position, Command. HVT and his security detail are down, hostage secure, charges set. Too many hostiles, we're ready to proceed." We needed to level this fucking compound.

"Hold your position, Alpha," Command ordered as gunfire erupted through the shattered windows from the adjacent building. "Incoming intel on building two. Possible second HVT."

Zulu came up beside me with the blindfolded hostage who had his hands zip-tied behind his back. Echo and Delta followed, still picking off a few squirters.

Billy brought up the rear. "What are we waiting for?"

"Intel from Command." I tipped my chin toward building two. "Possible second HVT."

"No easy day." Bravo smiled, already turning toward the building. "Cover me, Zulu."

"Copy that." Zulu dropped to a crouch and sighted his rifle.

My comms crackled, and Command came back on the line. "Alpha, mission incomplete. Building two has a second HVT. *Repeat*, building two has a second HVT. Hold for description and exact location."

"Good copy, Command," I replied before stopping Billy. "Hold position, Bravo. Waiting on sitrep from Command."

Billy glanced over his shoulder. "I'll get the intel sooner. Sixy seconds. One sweep and I'll know who we're after."

I didn't disagree, the terrorists protected their higher-ups. If there were any HVTs in that building, there'd be a security detail around them. But chain of command was chain of command. "Wait," I ordered, as three shots hit right above my head, pinging off building one.

The hostage dropped to the dirt as Delta and Echo spun and started firing.

Ducking low, Billy pointed out the obvious. "We don't have time to wait."

A halo of rounds from the convoy showered over our position, and the hostage cried out as he took one in the leg.

Fuck this. "I'm going in," I told Billy. "You and Zulu cover me."

"I got this one, Alpha." Billy held his fist out to me. "Just relay the intel from Command when you get it, and remember the promise."

I fist bumped him and gave him our standing promise even thought he didn't need to remind me of it. "I promise I'll take care of her if you kick your last door down." I'd always take care of Emmy.

Billy held my stare and gave me his usual warning. "You better, or I'll come back and beat your ass before kicking your ass."

Before I pulled the trigger with my first shots of cover fire, Billy was already double-timing it toward the adjacent building. Kicking in the southeast door, he disappeared inside.

"Alpha, *hold*, we—"

I didn't hear the rest of the transmission from Command.

Building two exploded.

Flames shooting into the air, the blastwave threw everyone back.

Rubble rained down.

THANK YOU!

Thank you so much for reading SEAL! Turn the page for a preview of ALPHA, the first heart-pounding, page-turning, exciting standalone book in the Alpha Elite Series!

ALPHA

Billionaire.

Mercenary.

Navy SEAL.

The Teams trained me to be a killer. War taught me to be ruthless. Then an ill-fated mission proved I was human. Combat wounded, cut loose by the Navy, I had a choice. Fade into obscurity or use the skills I had.

Alpha Elite Security was born, and three years later, my company was the most sought-after security contractor in the world. Five global locations, ten company jets, every one of my employees military trained—we were the best of the best. Overseeing operations, I didn't have time for women or anything other than growing my company. My success rate unmatched, I'd never lost a client.

Then I got a call, the only call that would get me back in the field. She was missing. The woman I'd left behind seven years ago. Now I had one objective.

Code name: Alpha.
Mission: Extraction.

ALPHA is the first standalone book in the exciting Alpha Elite Series by USA Today Bestselling author, Sybil Bartel. Come meet Adam "Alpha" Trefor and the dominant, alpha heroes who work for AES!

PREVIEW OF ALPHA

The Alpha Elite Series
By Sybil Bartel

Adam

MY ATTENTION ALREADY SHOT, THE VIBRATION AGAINST MY leg was only an excuse. Discreetly reaching into my pants pocket, I slid out my cell and read the text.

Calling in ten seconds. Answer.

I glanced at my friend and employee, Zane "Zulu" Silas, and tipped my chin toward the door.

Speaking to three executives from a Fortune 100 company that was having supply issues with one of their manufacturing facilities because it was in a hot zone, Zulu didn't falter in his assurance that we could eliminate their problem as he nodded at me.

"Gentlemen, if you'll please excuse me, an urgent matter has come up." I stood. "Mr. Silas will be able to answer any of your questions and give you a schedule of our fees. Thank you for reaching out to Alpha Elite Security. We look forward to your business."

My cell already buzzing with an incoming call, I walked out of the conference room on the forty-seventh floor of AES's Manhattan headquarters.

Striding into my corner office, I shut the glass door and answered the call. "What's up?"

"I'm your best fucking friend is what's up," Vance Conlon, my first hire, boasted.

My best friend was dead. "Because?" I demanded.

"Because I'm having fun with your newly updated proprietary face-recognition software."

Staring at a skyline I hated, I didn't bite.

"You going to ask how much fun?" he taunted.

"No." He'd tell me. Vance never called unless he had something to say. "And it's not proprietary. We're testing it for the military, and you're not supposed to have access to it yet."

"Okay, Alpha, you win, I give." Vance chuckled. "I found her. Twenty-five minutes ago, she walked out of JFK and got in a cab. And for the record, I don't give a shit whose software it is. If you didn't want me using it, you shouldn't have put it on the servers."

The air kicked out of my chest, and I leaned against my desk for support. "What else?"

"Right, you knew I wouldn't stop there." I could practically hear him gloat before his tone turned all business. "Anyway, speaking of software, I hacked the cab company and tracked her. The driver has his GPS set for a small grocery mart near her co-op. If you leave the office now, you can get there before she's done shopping for cheap white wine—Californian at least—dark chocolate, and mild salsa. Which if you ask me, the latter is sacrilegious and the first is just in poor taste."

"Do I want to know how you know her shopping list?"

"Do you want to know how I know you're leaning against your desk looking like you've just had your ass kicked?" he countered.

Goddamn it. Glancing up, I scanned the bookshelf in front of me. "I'm sweeping my office after we hang up."

"Yes, do that," he replied absently as he typed on his computer from wherever the hell he was today. "Check the lobby and the conference room while you're at it. Let me know what you find."

"I'm going to regret introducing you to November, aren't I?" Nathan "November" Rhys was the best cybersecurity specialist I knew. The Air Force's loss was my gain when he went civilian.

"No, but you're going to regret not grabbing a car in the next three minutes if you want to stalk that market and see her."

I didn't comment. Vance knew the drill. I didn't see her, ever.

I looked out for her, kept tabs on her travel, and occasionally checked her bank account balance to make sure she didn't need anything—but I purposely never crossed paths with her.

Vance gave me an exaggerated sigh. "Right. No contact. And why is that exactly?" The question rhetorical, he didn't wait for an answer. "Oh, that's right, because you have no balls."

I stared out at skyscrapers and miles of grayness. I didn't want to admit my control was slipping. It'd been years. Her life was different. Mine was... *fuck*, really different.

Except it wasn't.

I was still flying in jets, chasing down bad guys and collecting a paycheck for people shooting at me. I just wasn't doing it for the Navy as a SEAL anymore. Regardless, Vance had a point. Time had passed, and seven years of hard-practiced resolve was wearing me down.

"Tell you what," Vance continued, "I'm going to read into your silence, and...." He trailed off as he typed. "There. A service not affiliated with AES just had a drop-off at your location. The driver's swinging around, and he'll be downstairs in thirty seconds. Since this isn't one of our own, no one will be the wiser. Go lurk in the shadows. You're good at that. Or walk the fuck up to her. I don't care, just lay eyes on her. For all we know, it'll be three weeks again before I spot her, and maybe seeing her will change your attitude."

I didn't say no. I hesitated.

Then I was walking.

The phone still to my ear, my feet moving, I hit the call button for the elevator before I could tell myself everything I'd built wasn't for her or the opportunity of this moment. "I don't have an attitude."

"Yes, you do." Vance chuckled as the doors opened

immediately. "You have an attitude that says you haven't been laid this side of the decade. Also, you're welcome for the waiting lift."

Christ. "Did you hack the building's security for this or call in a favor with the guys in the command room?"

"Unlike sailors, a Marine never tells."

Ignoring his Navy versus Marines jab, I stepped into the elevator that I normally would've had to wait for. "This is a mistake."

Vance's usual casual tone turned somber. "We've all made mistakes. Walking into a grocery store in Manhattan doesn't come close to making the list, but regret does. Go see this woman, Trefor. It's time." He hung up.

Adrenaline filled my veins like a fix. A fix I only got from two things in life. But it'd been years since my last HALO on the Teams, and even longer since I'd seen her. Two addictions, and neither one curable.

I'd left the Teams, but I'd never left her.

Impatient, I watched the last few floors tick down on the display, and a moment later the doors slid open to the busy lobby. Stalking across the polished floors and out the revolving doors, I made my way to a black Town Car double-parked in front of the building.

Opening the rear passenger door, the driver, an older gentleman, smiled. "Good evening. Mr. Adam Trefor, I assume?"

I nodded in acknowledgment even though after years of

being a civilian, it was still odd to hear people call me Adam instead of Alpha. "Do you know where we're going?"

"Yes, sir."

"Hurry," I demanded.

"Of course, sir." He shut my door, but he didn't hurry. He couldn't. It was fucking Manhattan at eighteen hundred hours on a Thursday.

Thirteen punishing minutes later, he pulled in front of one of those small, overpriced delis that doubled as a grocery store for basic needs that Manhattan was infamous for. Before I could get out of the car, my cell vibrated with a new text.

Perfect timing, she's still inside. Last aisle by the white wines. But grab the Peju Province. You can thank me later.

Vowing to find a new assignment for Vance the second I was back in the office, I glanced at the driver. "Can you circle the block until I come back out?"

"Of course, sir. Take all the time you need."

"Thank you." With a nod, I was out of the car and buttoning the jacket of my custom Ermenegildo Zegna suit as I aimed for the front door of the market.

Ignoring the glances from women shopping by themselves, I cut across the front of the store and rounded the corner on the last aisle.

Then I stopped dead in my tracks.

Jesus.

Blonde, ethereal, delicate, and more beautiful than I

remembered, the only woman I'd ever loved stood mere feet away from me in a pale green dress.

Staring, my heart pounding, the air in my lungs nonexistent, all I could think was how unforgivably selfish I'd been on the worst day of her life.

I deserved her hate, but I told myself that was seven years ago. Time was on my side, and it'd been long enough. She had to forgive me.

Move, Trefor.

Make the move.

As if sensing my presence, she suddenly looked over her shoulder, her gaze landing exactly where I stood.

But she didn't look up at me.

Not all the way.

Her head slightly dipped, her gaze cast down as if staring at my legs, her emerald green eyes didn't meet mine.

Fuck this.

I stepped forward.

The man came around the corner from the opposite end of the aisle. Dark haired, bearded, he smiled wide and kissed her cheek. She looked surprised, but she let him take the basket that was perched on top of her small rolling suitcase and the bottle of wine from her hand.

Turning to the shelves of red zins in front of me, I tried to ignore the strike to my chest that wasn't at all like the goddamn kick I'd felt in my office. This was a full-blown, direct hit IED.

Leveled to nothing but shrapnel, I stood there.

I just fucking stood there.

Rooted like a coward, I watched the asshole put the wine back on the shelf and dump the basket on the floor. Taking her suitcase and smiling again as he spoke to her, he nodded toward the front of the store.

She said something I couldn't hear.

He threw his head back and laughed.

Not even cracking a smile, she listened as he spoke again.

Then she nodded, and they both turned toward my position.

I didn't hesitate.

I turned the corner, crossed the front of the store, and walked out.

To find out what happens next,
grab your copy of ALPHA!

ABOUT THE AUTHOR

Sybil Bartel is a *USA Today* Bestselling author of unapologetic alpha heroes. Whether you're reading her deliciously dominant mercenaries, bodyguards or military heroes, all of her heart-stopping, page-turning romantic suspense novels have sexy-as-sin alpha heroes!

Sybil resides in South Florida and she is forever Oliver's mom.

To find out more about Sybil Bartel or her books, please visit her at:

Website: sybilbartel.com

Facebook page: www.facebook.com/sybilbartelauthor

Facebook group: www.facebook.com/
groups/1065006266850790

Instagram: www.instagram.com/sybil.bartel

Twitter: twitter.com/SybilBartel

BookBub:www.bookbub.com/authors/sybil-bartel

Newsletter: http://eepurl.com/bRSE2T

Printed in Great Britain
by Amazon

43002202R00046